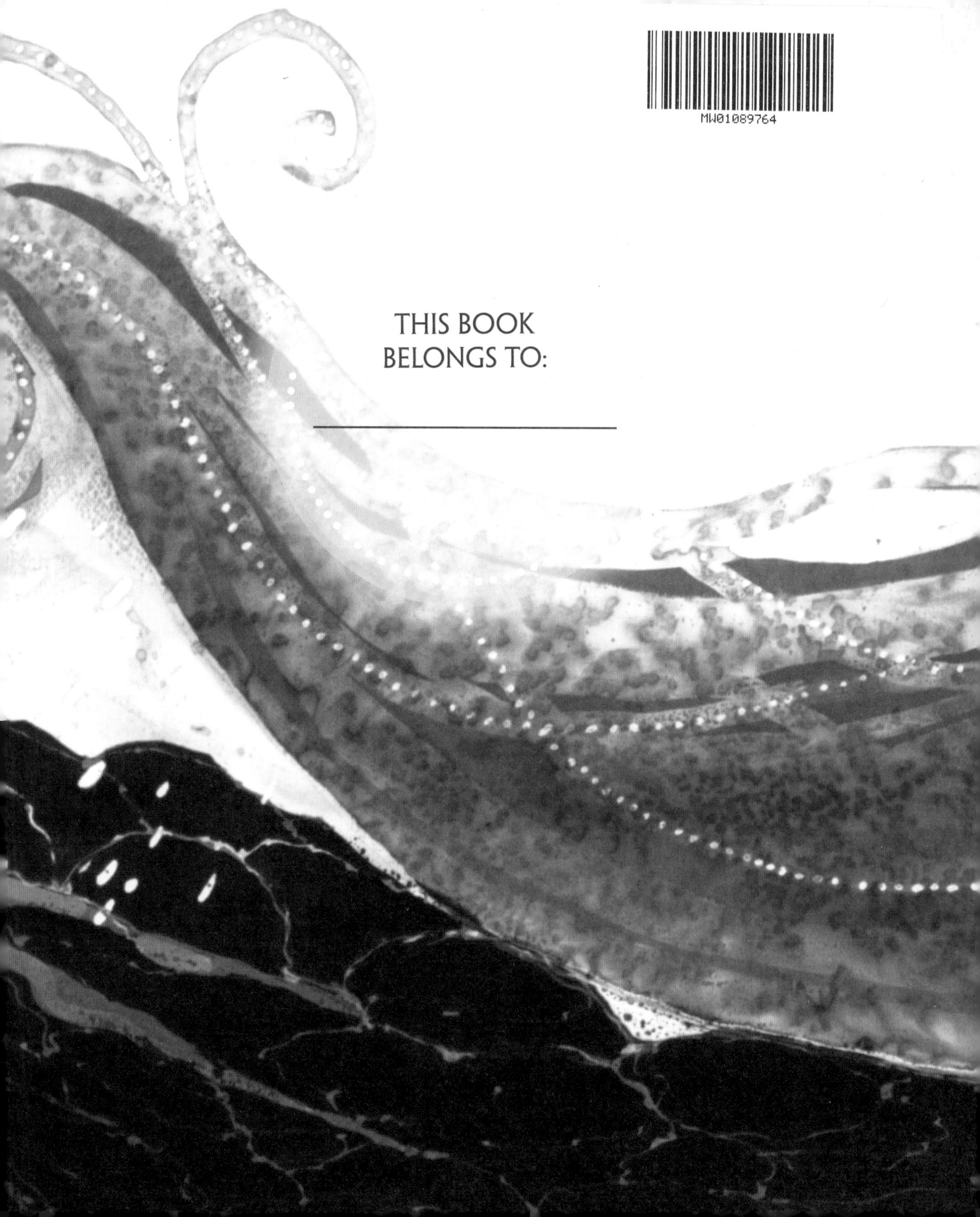
THIS BOOK
BELONGS TO:
MW01089764

PELE AND POLI'AHU

A Tale of Fire and Ice

Retold by Malia Collins

Illustrated by Kathleen Peterson

Long, long ago, on the Island of Hawai‘i, there lived two beautiful goddesses. Pele, the goddess of fire, lived on the slopes of Mauna Loa. Poli‘ahu, the goddess of snow, lived on the snowcapped peaks of Mauna Kea.

Each of them wore great cloaks. Pele's cloak was fire red. Poli'ahu's was the icy color of snow. Separated from each other, they stayed on their own mountaintop until one day when Pele decided to create some mischief.

It was a beautiful crisp day. A perfect day for sledding. Poli‘ahu and her snow goddesses Līlīnoe, Waiau, and Kahoupokāne carried their hōlua, sleds made from koa, down the snowy slopes of Mauna Kea to a soft green hillside above Hāmākua. All of them were very skilled riders, but Poli‘ahu was the best.

When it was her turn to race, she leapt onto her sled and flew down the hill, quickly passing her friends. When the others finally made it to the bottom of the hill, they found Poliʻahu patiently waiting.

As they began to climb the hillside to race again, a beautiful young woman appeared out of nowhere. Her dark red dress was the color of lava and the haku lei she wore was made from the delicate blossoms of the ʻōhiʻa lehua tree. The snow goddesses whispered to each other, "Who is this stranger?"

The stranger asked if she could join in their races. The snow goddesses, eager for a new challenger, nodded yes. “Hele mai,” they said. “Come and join us.”

They were excited to race the woman in red. Līlīnoe handed the stranger her hōlua. Once at the top, the stranger set the sled down, ready to race each maiden. Poliʻahu smiled and watched.

The beautiful stranger jumped on her sled and raced each snow maiden down the hillside. Three times she raced and three times she won. Confident, the stranger then turned to Poliʻahu. "Do you dare try and race me?" Poliʻahu smiled and glanced up toward the mountain. "If it is a greater challenge you want, let us race from higher ground—past where the snow meets the grass." The stranger agreed with a smirk.

Both racers swooped down the mountain, their hair flying behind them in the wind, their strong legs crouched low and tight on the sleds. The stranger could hear the sound of Poliʻahu's sled barreling down the hill. She and Poliʻahu kept close together, the noses of their sleds lunging ever closer to the finish.

In the end, Poliʻahu, who had raced this slope many, many times, pulled ahead and proved too fast for the stranger, beating her to the edge of the ocean that lay at the bottom of the hill.

The beautiful stranger grew very angry. She threw her sled far over the hillside. Her dark eyes turned a stormy black. Her red cape crackled against her skin. The skies overhead began burning yellow, then orange, then red. Poli‘ahu watched in amazement as the stranger began to change right before her eyes.

The air around them went from warm to hot. Poli‘ahu could feel the heat rising in her blood. The hillside they stood on, just seconds ago so lush and green, began to dry up. Flowers wilted, trees turned black and crisp, leaves dropped to the ground and sizzled. The mountain started to shake and pulse like it was coming back to life.

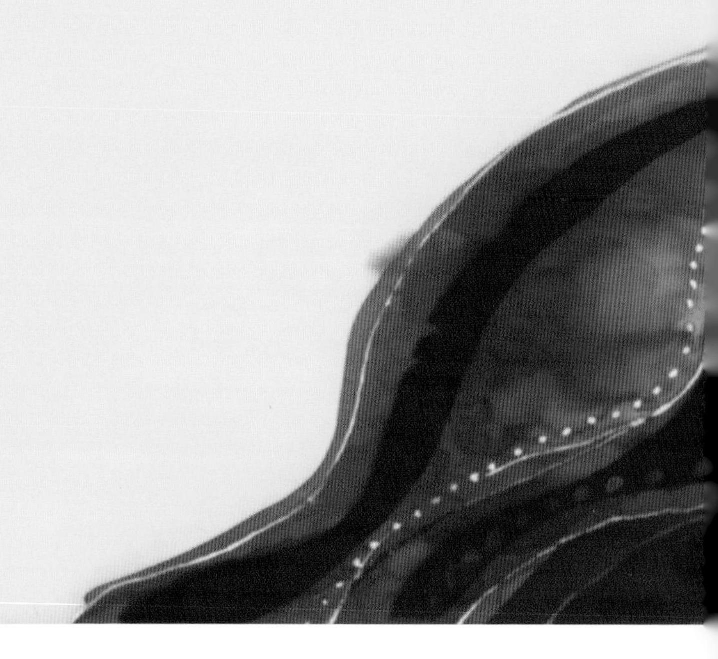

Beneath her feet, Poli‘ahu could feel the earth growing hotter and hotter. Suddenly she knew the stranger was her archenemy Pele, the goddess of fire.

Pele lifted her arms, calling out to the volcano. Cracks in the earth appeared and yawned wide open. Great rivers of lava boiled up out of the ground. The sound the earth made as it shifted and broke open was like nothing the snow goddesses had heard before.

Swift-moving lava raced down the mountainsides, splitting into many smaller and faster streams. Billowy steam clouds reached high toward the heavens. Snow and ice melted. Poliʻahu's icy white kingdom was disappearing before her eyes.

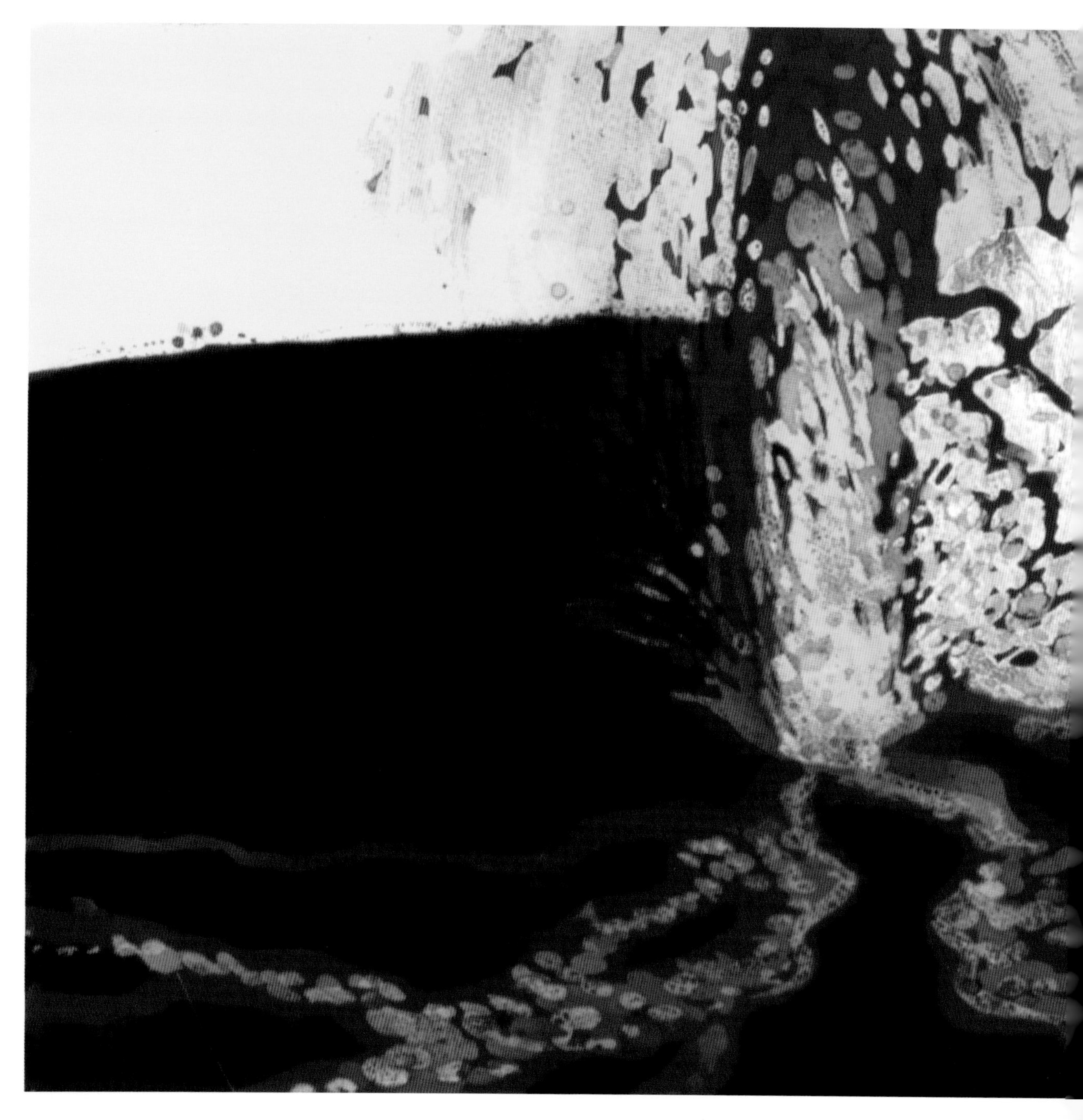

Poli'ahu hurried up the slopes as quickly as she could go. From down below, Pele threw spears of red-hot lava that melted the snow and ice. The edges of Poli'ahu's white cloak began to burn up. She could feel the fire against her heels. She ran faster and faster.

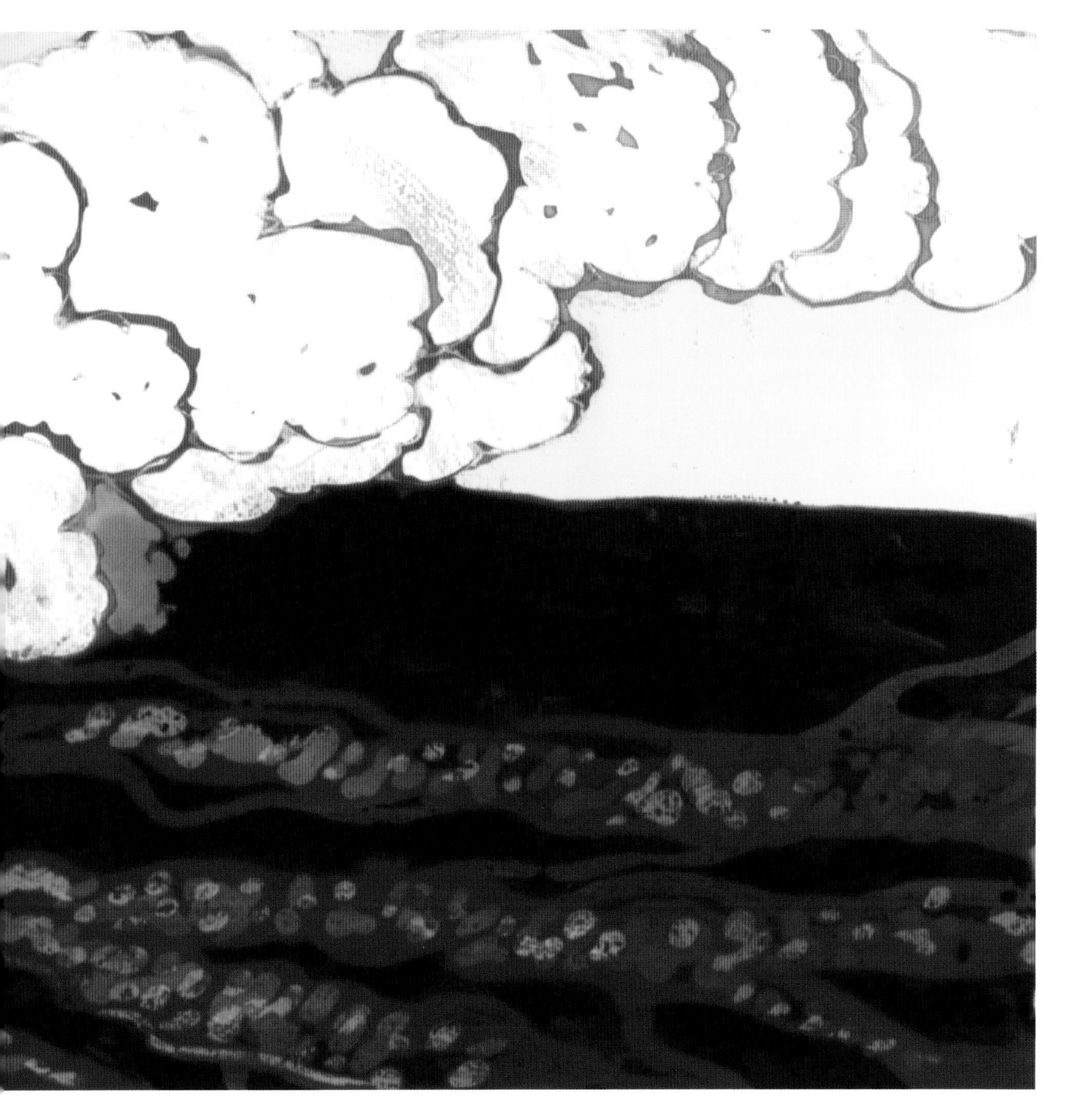

ʻPele stormed on, now throwing giant balls of hot lava at Poliʻahu's cloak. Poliʻahu gathered ıer cloak behind her and jumped from side to side, barely missing the trails of lava that tried o block her path home.

Once Poli‘ahu reached the top of the mountain, she turned around to see what Pele had done. Lava flowed as far as the eye could see. The ocean boiled and steam hung over the bay in fat yellow clouds.

Even though her strong legs and arms were tired from sledding and running, Poliʻahu was able to summon every ounce of strength she had left. She lifted her great white cloak and threw it over the peak of the mountain, just like she was throwing a gigantic net out to sea. Her cloak floated and then spread out over the top of the mountain.

Earthquakes shook from below. Rivers of lava and waves of snow clashed beneath the sky. Pele could feel Poliʻahu's chill spread across the mountain. She tried to melt the snow with lava. She called for steam and fire to blow up from the ground, but it was no match for the power of Poliʻahu's snow and ice.

Pele's red rivers froze. White snowflakes fell from above and put out the fires. Pele watched, helpless, as Poli'ahu's cloak unfolded and covered the mountain in white. All that was left of Pele's fury were the narrow strips of black lava that stretched out into the blue sea.

Pele shivered in the icy air. She looked at the white mountaintop that shimmered in the sunlight. Streams of melted snow ran down the sides of the mountains into the valleys below. On the hillside where they raced their sleds, the trees once again bloomed lush and green. Pele knew she had been defeated. She gave up her battle and headed down the mountain, back to her hot and smoldering home that lay in the southern part of the island.

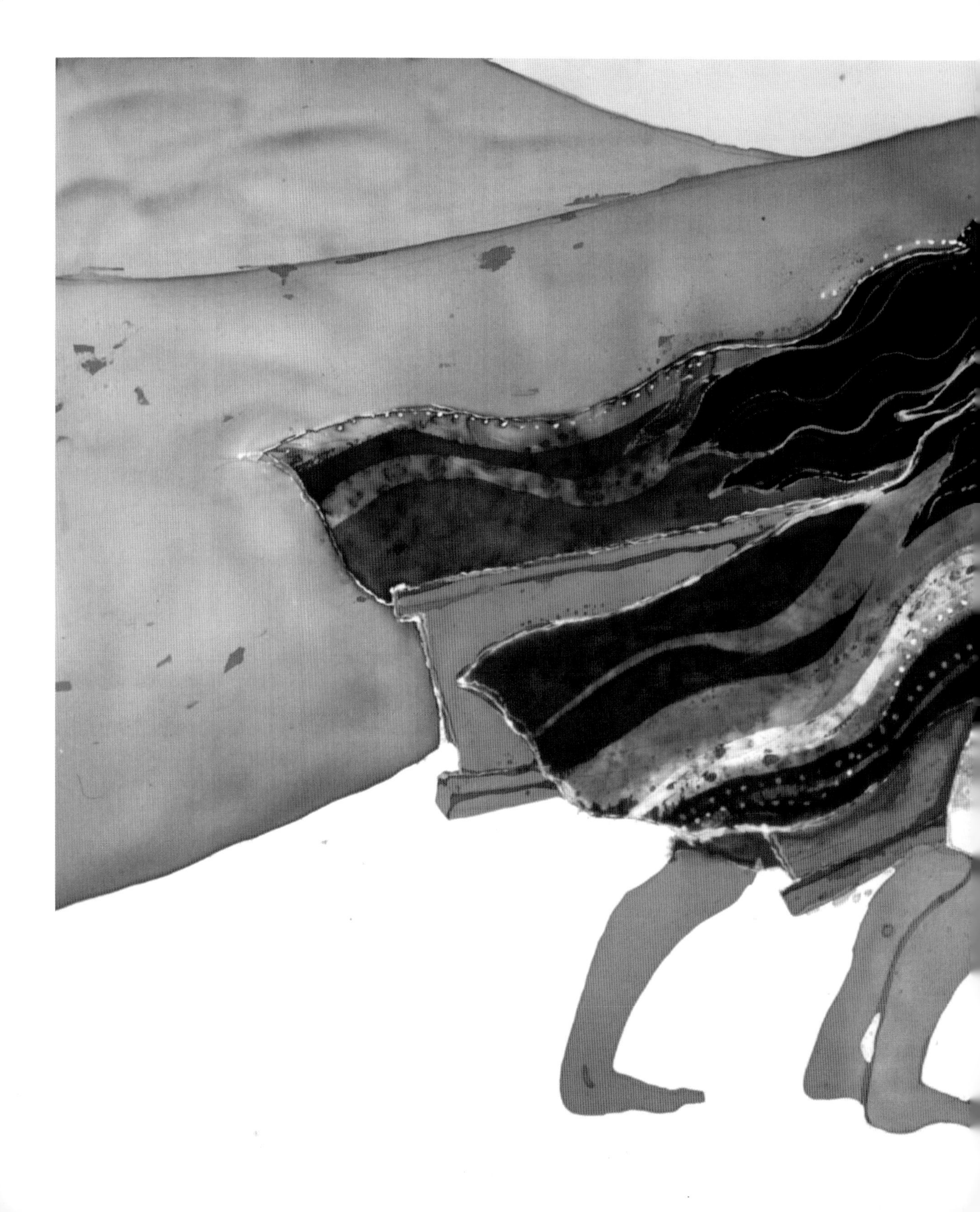

Poli'ahu looked at her friends. "Let's go home," she said. They gathered their sleds and hiked back up the slopes of Mauna Kea. When they reached the summit, the snow maidens turned back toward the sea. From where they stood they could see where Pele lived. They knew, although she had been defeated, it was not the last they would hear from her.

Even to this day, Pele tries to take over Poli'ahu's side of the island. But as long as Poli'ahu reigns, and as long as the snow maidens keep their mountaintop cool, the Island of Hawai'i is able to live in peace.

ABOUT THE AUTHOR

Malia Collins, born and raised in Kailua on the Island of O'ahu, is a writer, editor, and teacher currently living in Idaho with her husband, Josh, and two children, Max and Mehana. She served as editor of *The Hawai'i Review* and *The Idaho Review,* has been published in a number of magazines, and contributed to a series of books about Hawai'i. Collins was inspired to write children's books about Hawai'i to introduce her children to their heritage.

ABOUT THE ILLUSTRATOR

Kathleen B. Peterson has illustrated twenty-one books. She is the founding director of the Central Utah Art Center and displays her landscape paintings in galleries around the West and on the Big Island of Hawai'i. A past resident of Hawai'i, Peterson currently divides her time between Utah and Idaho. Her other BeachHouse children's books are: *Koa's Seed, Moon Mangoes,* and *'Iwalani's Tree.*

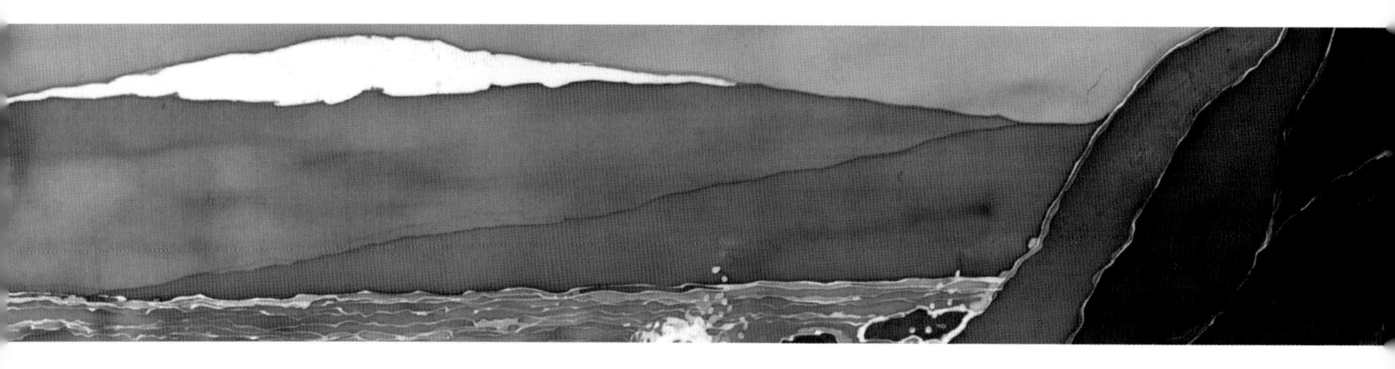

Originally printed in 2005 in a larger format.

Library of Congress Control Number: 2018946087

ISBN 978-1-949000-03-0
First Printing, August 2018
Second Printing, March 2020

BeachHouse Publishing, LLC
PO Box 5464
Kāne'ohe, Hawai'i 96744
email: info@beachhousepublishing.com
www.beachhousepublishing.com

Printed in by RRD Dongguan, China 1/2020

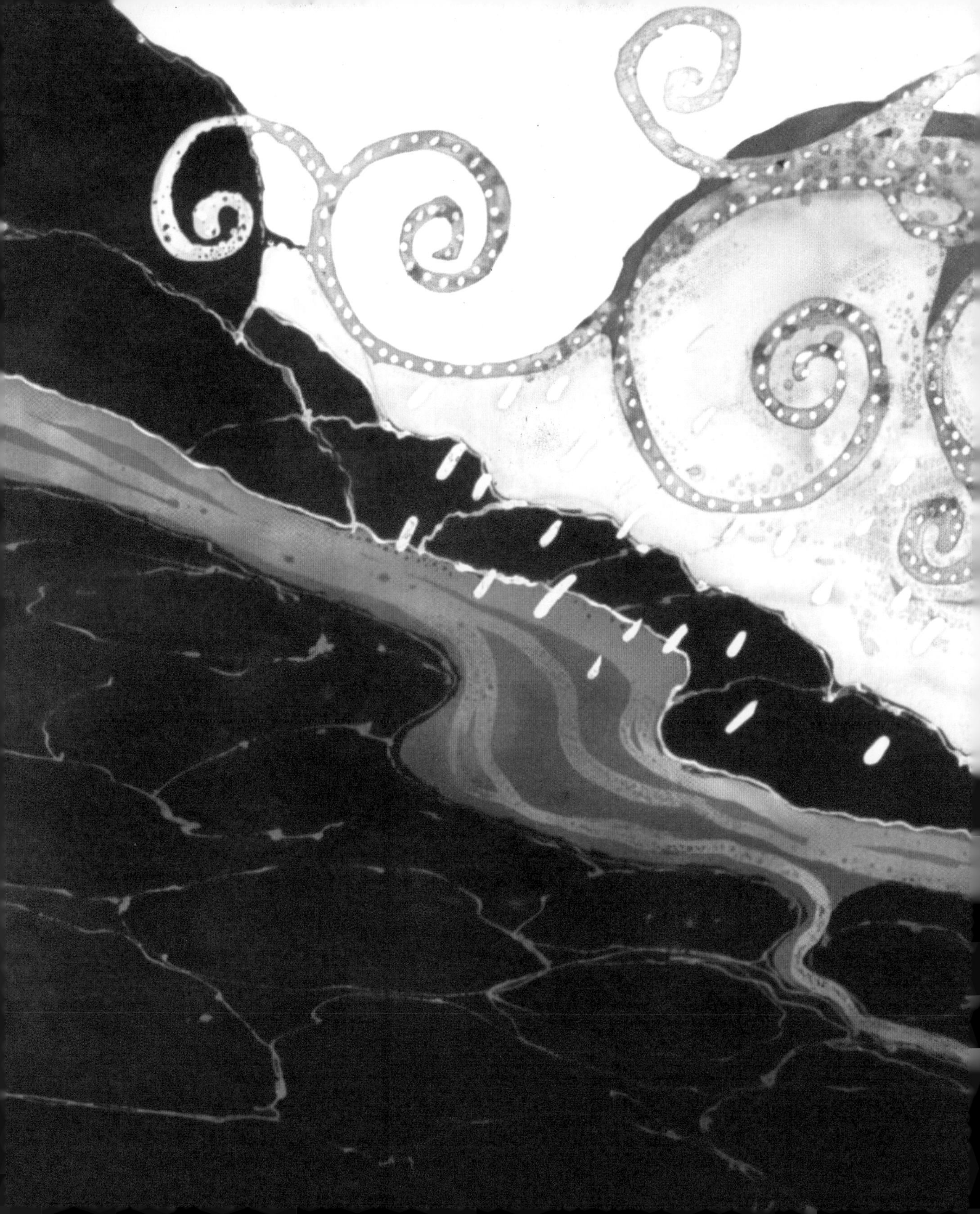